Fascinating Short Stories Of Boys Who Never Gave Up

* * *

Dally Perry

Cover Design by
Victichy

SMARTARROW PUBLISHER

Smart Arrow Publishers

www.Dallybooks.com

Publisher's Note: This is a work of fiction. Names, characters, places, and incidents are a product of the author's imagination. Locales and public names are sometimes used for atmospheric purposes. Any resemblance to actual people, living or dead, or to businesses, companies, events, institutions, or locales is completely coincidental.

Book and cover design © 2022 By Victichy

Ordering Information: Special discounts are available on quantity purchases by corporations, associations, and others. For details, contact the publisher via email drewdallybooks@gmail.com

First Edition

ISBN 978-1-956677-40-9

Printed in the United States of America

Contents

For Valen, Vishal, and Videl.

Introduction

We all love stories, especially those that teach us morals. We recall stories about the friendly animal kingdom and how their various attributes earned them their place in the kingdom. Popular animals in these stories were the lion (king of the jungle), the tortoise (the slowest but most intelligent), and the elephant (the biggest animal in the kingdom with the best memory).

Stories have a way of teaching us salient principles of life, correct us when we err, and help to shape our destiny and how best we ought to approach life issues in general.

Stories help to offer in-depth insights that enable us to face life issues head on by taking preemptive measures. Stories come in handy all through our lives because challenges don't ever take a break, leaving us to consistently tackle them and move on to the next to proffer solutions.

Stories are adopted in the educational system today because research has it that storytelling helps to quicken understanding among children in several subject matters. I am positive that this collection of interesting stories will not only entertain, inspire, and educate you, but will also help you connect with your inner-self, leading to self-development, personal growth, and personal awareness

$$* \overset{*}{\underset{*}{}}$$

2

BRAVERY

The Old Withering Tree And The Homeless Bird

Adversities can bring about growth

There was once an old withering tree in the middle of an isolated desert. It no longer had leaves, but fragile branches that served as a home to an attractive bird named Whistle. One day, a strong wind blew and pulled the tree from its roots. This rendered Whistle homeless with no other option than to look for a new home.

Whistle had to go in search of a new shelter and flew tirelessly for several miles. Then Whistle got depressed by this search and felt that life had turned against it and a grave calamity had befallen it. After flying for many days, Whistle was tired and had almost lost hope, and then ahead was a forest filled with trees. This gave Whistle countless options to choose from in order to build a new home.

This story teaches us that problems will surely come, and no one might be available to help you out of it. This is your faith being tested. So, make the best out of every challenge and approach challenges with a positive mindset. In life, things may not always go as planned. Know that not all the challenges come to destroy you, some come to make you stronger and bring enlightenment. Challenges come to pave the way for a better life. They are just temporary.

Captain Scott And The Deadly Snow Storm

Draw strength from your weakness

Once there lived a captain named Scott. He hailed from England. Sadly, Captain Scott died on his way to the South Pole in a terrible snow storm. His body was later discovered, and on him was found an incomplete letter addressed to James Barrie – a renowned English writer. The last word in the note was "Courage."

The popular English writer saved the letter with great pride in a coffin as a relic of the valiant warrior. Years later, James Barrie was in a terrible accident that claimed the use of his right hand, which happened to be his greatest strength. This paused his creativity and all his work couldn't continue. This put the writer in a depressed state for many months. He later looked at the casket that contained the letter and miraculously, it gave him strength and hope.

It is wise to know that positive words give strength to the weak and encourage the downtrodden.

Set The Man Right And The World Will Align

Focus on what is right

Once upon a time, there lived a harsh disciplinarian who was a father to a very intelligent but naughty girl named Mary. On one fateful day, the father was trying to work but Mary kept getting in the way. He thought of getting something to keep her occupied while he worked. So, he tore up a world map he found in a newspaper and gave it to Mary to arrange it carefully back together. In no time, she finished the task and went back to her dad. In his amazement, he inquired how Mary finished so soon and she said there was a man's image behind the world map, so when she set the man right, the world map came together too.

Life will attempt to multiply your struggles, instead work on your mindset first and the majority of the job is done. Distraction will come, but it is not enough to take your gaze off your life goal. When you focus on the right things, the world will fall in place.

* 8 *

The Scary Underground Train Crash

Look your fear in the face

Once upon a time, there was a terrible accident in February 1975 that claimed the life of 41 people after an underground train crashed against a stony wall at the Moorgate station in London. Part of those critically injured was Margaret – a 19-year-old policewoman. She laid on the floor, one of her legs beneath her body, trapped under a huge steel girder.

In the midst of the dead bodies surrounding Margaret, she tried to show bravery by helping a man up, but none of them could move because that would cause further pain. Margaret lost her left leg because she lost so much blood and had to get it amputated.

Margaret faced her fears. She was in so much pain, but still attempted to save a life. Margaret is a role model, displaying genuine acts of kindness and humanity to others. Despite her appalling predicament, she was still positive. She kept her humor intact despite her circumstances. Margaret's positive spirit is an enviable virtue worth emulating. It's good to free oneself of fear and embrace courage, don't soak yourself in your troubles. Your life is not hopeless.

Satan And His Messenger

Don't be discouraged

On one fateful sunny day, Satan was busy roaming the streets aimlessly with his ugly dogs; hunting dogs who hid in the shadows. His dogs were known in the vicinity for their mischievousness and popularly called "little mischievous devils of human frailty."

While Satan was making his rounds on this beautiful day, he met a man named Ragu walking down the street. Satan then instructed one of his dogs to go to Ragu and preach discouragement to him. The ugly looking dog ran off obediently, crossed over to Ragu quietly, and whispered softly to him "You are discouraged!" but Ragu responded that he wasn't.

This time, the dog spoke louder and more insistently, until Ragu admitted to being discouraged. The dog was overjoyed that he had defeated Ragu, who was now sad and downcast. The dog returned to Satan, his master, and told him how scared Ragu's face was when he encountered him, and how Ragu scampered away in fright like a scared cat.

Soon enough, Satan spotted another man named Ramu and Satan instructed that the dog go again and preach discouragement to him. The dog whispered to Ramu, saying, "You are discouraged and you know it." Ramu refused to accept what the dog said and replied, "I am not discouraged." The dog was more fierce the second time he told Ramu he must be discouraged, but Ramu refused to listen. Then the dog raised his voice at Ramu, saying, "You are discouraged, Ramu. Accept it." But guess what happened? Ramu raised his voice louder and told the dog, "I am not discouraged, you are and you are a liar."

This statement broke the dog down and he went back to Satan, his master, where he relayed everything that transpired. The dog told Satan, "Ramu told me he can never be discouraged, called me a liar, and forbade me to never come close to him again. Master, now I am the one who is discouraged."

Life will always paint a false picture of you to you, the wicked will also send dogs to derail you from your vision, but don't give in to the challenges that come your way, no matter what. Always speak words of affirmation.

The truth always hurts. Telling someone the true situation of a thing or what they really are is upsetting. We get upset when our bad sides or limitations are called out. The same goes when good qualities are recognized as well, so be careful how you approach things.

The Brave Boy Bold Enough To Wish

Bravery isn't the absence of fear

As Derick Brighton circled across the hall from his class, he bumped into a tall skinny boy who was running in the opposite direction from the fifth grade.

"Watch where you are going, dummy," the skinny-looking boy shouted as he attempted not to knock down Derick, who was just a little third grader.

With a sneer on the fifth-graders' face, he held his right leg and imitated the manner in which Derick limped away. Derick shut his eyes, trying to avoid looking his way. He went back to his classroom, but kept thinking about how the tall skinny boy mocked him.

But funny enough, the tall skinny boy wasn't the only one who teased him since he got to the third grade. In fact, Derick could recount that for every single day, someone teased him and got away with it. It was either he was teased for his incoherent speech or his limping. Derick was sad and fed up with it all, the constant teasing made him withdraw into his shell, and he felt all alone in a classroom filled with his other classmates.

After school that day, Derick made his way back home quietly. On getting home, it was time for dinner. Derick was so quiet and his mum (Grace Brighton) got wind that things weren't going well at her son's school, but thankfully she came bearing some exciting news to break the sad air that had been clouding the dinner table.

Grace Brighton told her son, "There is a Christmas wish competition on the radio, write a letter to Santa and you stand a chance to win a prize. I strongly think someone at this table will surely win."

Derick laughed and said, "This competition sounds like fun." His thoughts started running wild, and he thought to himself what he'd love for Christmas. Derick was overjoyed at the thought that he'd been given a rare opportunity to ask Santa for a gift and he had faith that his letter would be chosen to be granted amongst the lot.

He picked up his pen and paper and started to scribble down words while his family wondered what in the world he would ask for. His father thought he'd ask for a puzzle book, while his mother guessed a huge toy car much bigger than his last Christmas present... but these were Derick's words in the letter to Santa. He started by saying...

Dear Santa Claus,

My name is Derick and I am nine years old. I have a challenge at my school. Please can you help me, Santa? Kids at my school mock me because of the way I talk, walk, and run. I have cerebral palsy. All I ask is to experience one day where no one will mock me or make fun of me.

With Love,

Derick.

Back at the radio station, Famous Dial in Canandaigua, Ontario, they kept receiving a whole bunch of letters for the Christmas wish competition. The workers at the radio station had a great time reading various Christmas wishes from girls and boys from all over the city. When the manager of the Radio station, Brad Clarkson, read Derick's letter, he understood that cerebral palsy was a muscle condition that bewildered Derick's classmates, who didn't understand Derick's disorder.

Mr. Brad Clarkson took it a step further and called up the local newspaper to tell everyone how brave a third-grader would be to make such a special and bold wish. The following day, Derick's picture, attached to his letter, was on the cover of the newspapers. Before you say "JACK!" the story had made the rounds all over the country. Newspapers and radio and television stations declared Derick as the remarkable little brave boy in Canandaigua, Ontario, who requested of Santa a rare Christmas present – a day without mocking.

Derick became famous overnight. He received a quantifiable number of letters everyday filled with holiday cheers and encouraging words from people all over the nation. Each of these letters were specially written for Derick. Over two thousand people extended a hand of support and friendship to him. Some shared their own disabilities with him and how they surmounted it.

Derick's joy knew no bounds, he felt genuine love. He saw the world in a different light. Derick then knew that the world was filled with people who cared for one another and no level of mockery would ever make him feel lonely in the world.

Derick was congratulated for his bravery to speak out. He was urged to ignore any form of teasing going forward and instead keep his chin up.

Derick had his wish of a peculiar day without teasing at his school. The school took it upon themselves to speak about the repercussions of bullying and how it made the bullied children feel. The mayor of the city proclaimed every December 21st as Derick Brighton Day, all through the city. The mayor thought Derick's request was simple, but it taught a vital lesson. "Every single person on earth deserves to be treated with dignity and respect," the mayor reiterated.

Marshall Bruce Mathers Iii (Eminem)

If your dream doesn't threaten you, then rethink it

When Eminem was just three months old, his father abandoned him and left his mother, Deborah, alone to raise Marshall (Eminem). Deborah had to do many odd jobs just to make ends meet and even moved out of their home to live at government housing projects or with relatives. They practically lived on government welfare to eat and live.

Eminem's full name is Marshall Bruce Mathers III, a renowned rapper, entertainment entrepreneur and songwriter. He was born to his parents, Deborah Mathers and Marshall Mathers, Jr., who were part of his band. Eminem, as he is popularly called, was born in Missouri in 1972.

Growing up, Marshall (Eminem) had it tough, as they constantly moved from one city to the other every four months for greener pastures. This made it hard for Deborah to build a proper home. Due to the challenges, Deborah developed paranoid personality disorder that didn't help the present situation, either. Marshall faced difficulty in school, did badly at his school work, and didn't have friends. He was bullied often and mocked by classmates.

When Marshall was twelve-years-old, they settled in Detroit. This neighborhood was predominantly African-American, with Marshall as a white face amongst the many blacks. The bullying increased, every day he was beat up by the black kids and his school grades suffered the most.

For every time Marshall tried to reach out to his father, he was rejected; calls and letters weren't responded to. But thank God for his uncle Ronnie Mathers. He played the role of a father to Marshall.

Marshall developed an interest in the English language, loved to read the dictionary and know the meaning of words, and reading comic books. At one point, he started writing his own comic books himself.

Marshall then fell in love with rap music after his uncle introduced the 1981 hit of Ice-T called "Reckless." His love for rap wasn't enough, so he went further to hone it by rhyming, writing rap verses, and stanzas. He spent ample time everyday getting better at writing and rhyming, but his grades suffered. He had to drop out of school after repeating three years in ninth grade.

From the age of fourteen, Marshall was consumed by his unending appetite for rap music and surrounded himself with things that fed that desire. His friends were young amateur rappers like him with a burning desire to be made rappers. He joined open mic nights for rap in Detroit.

In the midst of all these, Marshall had to work odd jobs, mostly at a restaurant, to assist his mum. He also welcomed his baby girl in 1995 by his girlfriend, Kimberly Scott. He decided to release a hip-hop album. A GBT production helped with his first album. The reaction of the populace to his album was demeaning, it wasn't accepted, and he was critiqued and compared to established rappers. In short, the local radio station didn't take the record and this hugely affected the sale of his album.

More misfortune hit. He was sacked from his job at the restaurant, and he turned to alcohol and drug abuse and tried to hurt himself, but didn't succeed. In his lowest point, he got up because his family needed his support and he went back to rapping. He channeled his anger to his rap lyrics and used his hard life to churn out a script. This informed the violent and angry real-life stories present in his songs. This carved a rap niche for Marshall that wasn't the norm amongst rappers who sing about unclad women, luxury cars, and wealth.

His second album, Slim Shady EP, was released in 1997 under Web Entertainment. This made a statement, as he got signed under Interscope Records by Dr. Dre.

Today Marshall (Eminem) has nothing less than thirteen Grammy Awards and is named the "Best Rapper" because his rap lyrics speaks about societal issues. He has his own radio station and recording label, a beautiful home, three kids (two adopted), and a loyal fan base who loves his craft.

Marshall didn't lose hope when his dream of becoming a rapper was questioned by all. He kept hope alive and adopted an "I cannot afford to fail" mindset that has set him apart today.

Marshall didn't let his miserable and pitiable past define the result of the future. He found a happy path in spite of his pain and rejection. Even though his first album was a failed sale, he didn't stop at one. Challenges didn't stop coming because he became famous or rich. He only built a stronger version of himself to withstand them when they came.

What's Up?

Don't take no for an answer

Jan Koum is the true classification of a hard worker and the creator of WhatsApp. He grew up as a pauper, very wretched in Ukraine. He struggled to keep food on the table and couldn't even afford running water.

Jan Koum discovered his skills in Silicon Valley and was close to being employed at Facebook, but didn't scale in the last part of the interview. He wasn't moody as a result, instead he moved on to create WhatsApp.

He was rejected at an interview he had been longing for all his life. He struggled to get the resources to create WhatsApp. People didn't believe in his dream until it materialized. He had to be hard working and diligent. He never accepted no for an answer.

In life, you need to have faith in yourself and keep your gaze on your goal.

The Most Rejected Man On Planet Earth

We all are born to do great things

Ever heard or seen the name Alibaba? It is one of the largest e-commerce platforms in China. Alibaba is owned by Jack Ma, who is the richest man in Asia. His net worth is close to $39 billion.

With the several rejections he faced all his life, he still didn't allow that to deter him in any way. The entrance of the internet in the mid 90's opened his eyes to many possibilities he never knew existed. With the internet, he has established many companies in spite of all the rejection he had experienced.

Jack Ma was rejected for the most part of his life. He was rejected from Harvard ten times. He was rejected from thirty jobs.

Jack detached himself from his past hurt so he could fly. He didn't look like he was advanced in age or not conversant with the use of the internet, but made the most of it.

Believe in you and don't let hurt get to you, it will only destroy you.

Starbucks Never Gave Up

Be consistent and resolute

He is the founder of Starbucks, which has become very famous today with a symbol very significant, like that of McDonalds, the crucifix, and even Superman. It was never this smooth for Howard, but consistency and steadfastness set him apart. Today, the Starbucks brand is a household name.

Howard Schultz visited over two hundred banks in search of a loan to float his business. He wasn't just looking for a loan for his business, but his wife was heavy with his first child. He was rejected many times during the year, but eventually was able to get a loan of $400,000 he needed from a doctor and two other individual investors.

Today, the Starbucks Company hires more than 137,000 people all around the world. Starbucks also has over 16,000 locations in forty different counties. As at 2010, this prestigious company has hired over 130,000 people, which is two times the population of Greenland. Since 1987, Starbucks has been adding two new stores every day.

Howard had to be consistent and resolute to achieve all Starbucks is today. Never give up, even though it seems hard. Howard persevered, that is why we are able to know an iconic brand like his.

Shoot For The Stars

Never aim low

The story of Ray Cros is a great perseverance story that shows that no one is a write off and success can take place at any given time in life.

The golden curves are similar to one of the largest, oldest, and most profitable businesses in the world. Ray Cros played a huge role in transforming McDonald's business into a global one. From a one location burger chain business in San Bernardino, it now has countless number of locations all over the world.

Ray Cros was a struggling fifty-year-old man back then. He worked as a milkshake machine salesman who lived from hand to mouth. One day, he woke up and said he wanted more from life. So, he met the brain behind McDonald's and made an offer to them about helping to grow their stagnant business. He eventually succeeded in convincing the brothers of a franchise model to expand the brand.

Ray Cros's idea resulted in a colossal expansion. They had to acquire more lands for different other locations for the business. That's how we all are able to know about McDonald's today.

Anyone's success can come any season of their life, all you have to do is to consistently work at improving yourself.

In life, don't be afraid of growing. When you take charge of your life and do what needs to be done, you don't only affect your life positively, but others around you.

Dream big. Without a dream to build a franchise, Mcdonalds would remain a burger joint consisting of one location.

Murphy Stephen's Lesson On Prejudice

We are all human with blood flowing through our veins

Murphy Stephen was Franklin's best friend during second grade. During Murphy's birthday celebration, all the boys in the classroom were always invited. Every day in school, excitement was always a topic of discussion.

His friend's would ask, "What kind of cake are you going to have?"

"Will your party have games with prizes?" "Will you have decorations of cartoon characters and will there be funny birthday caps?" Many questions showed how the boisterous lot would devour the party. All Murphy would do was smile and say, "Let's all wait and see."

All of Murphy's friends counted down to the long awaited birthday of their dear friend, which was that Saturday, as the invitation specified.

When the said date arrived, Franklin – Murphy's best friend – wrapped the gift he wanted to present to his friend, wore his best outfit, and waited for what seemed like eternity for his mum to shout, "It's time to move!"

Franklin was happy that he'd be the first to arrive at his best friend's birthday party because he intended to help arrange the place for the party. The table was decorated with Murphy's best cartoon characters like Superman, Super Mario, Batman, and Iron Man. It was a confluence of different cartoon characters, but it was beautiful though.

There were wooden banners of these same characters that looked real, so that any child could stand by it to take pictures, which looked beautiful. It appeared like a mini Disneyland or better still, Marvel Land. When all was set, Murphy's mum sent the boys to the front yard to wait for the other boys to arrive. Since Murphy lived on the edge of town and many of his friends hadn't visited before, it might be difficult for his friends to find his residence.

Murphy and Franklin sat on the steps and awaited their friends. They waited and waited but none of them came. Murphy began to cry like a little girl that was spanked. But finally, his mum came out and announced that the party would commence immediately. Murphy's mum ushered them in, tied a blindfold around their eyes and gave them a pin each with a tail and led them to the donkey taped to the wall. She said, "Whoever hits the tail nearest to the right place will win the very first super prize!" Franklin's tail ended near the donkey's nose while Murphy's own touched the right front hoof. This was so much fun as the boys laughed loudly.

Both Murphy and Franklin played all the games and shared all the super great prizes. There was so much cake to go round for the both of them and they both had extreme fun while the party lasted.

While Franklin was on his way home, he asked his mum, "Why didn't the other boys come? Murphy's birthday celebration was almost ruined."

Franklin's mum paused for a moment and said, "Darling, the other boys didn't come because Murphy is black."

Franklin protested back and said, "He's not black, his skin just looks tan all through the year." Franklin's mum responded, saying, "I know darling. You know that Murphy isn't like the others in your class, and some people are scared of those that don't look like them. People are prejudiced. They are prejudiced for no reason."

Franklin busted out, "Those boys are mean. How can they make Murphy so sad? I am never going to be prejudiced!" Franklin's mum gave him a warm hug and said, "That's great darling. It's a good thing that Murphy has a great friend in you."

The Lifesaving Chain Of Connection

We need each other to survive

It was during the summer after fourth grade that it dawned on Henry Joel that shared connection with others is vital for us to keep living.

Henry Joel screamed, "I am dying! I am dying!" Repeatedly as he hung on for his dear life. His toe slid out the space that was supporting him. With fear gripping him again, he screamed "I am dying!" Henry thought to himself, If I don't get a secure place to put my foot, I will fall. Henry used his feet to check around the surface for a place his foot would be secure. Just ahead through the steam, he could see his friend Peter kneeling above the pit.

Peter shouted, "Take my hand," and Henry stretched his hand far but couldn't grab Peter's hand, as sulfur had already filled his hands. Peter assured Henry, saying, "Be calm, I promise not to leave you, we'll get you out of here!"

Peter knelt by the steam vent, talking to Henry while the other boys scampered away to fetch help.

Henry knew that Peter would do everything within his power to save him. Their friendships grew out of the connection they had made in time past and the trust they had built with each other and while they were teammates in a soccer club.

They had learnt to communicate with each other while playing soccer with words like, "Your side," "Behind you," "Pass the ball!" and "Open over here."

Henry and Peter held the team as one for the entire year. That very summer, they were supposed to go to Singapore for the Big Cup Tournament. It was the very first time in a decade that their team representing their area would be given such an opportunity. But resources were the challenge to get themselves there. Their soccer team went in search of funds from the neighbors in the community and they were generously blessed. With the donations, they paid for their tournament fees and were on their way for an adventure of a lifetime.

On getting to the hotel, they practiced for hours. The next day, they went sight-seeing. After viewing nature's beauty, they passed by a steam vent, which is a crack within the earth's surface due to the pressure and the volcano's heat.

It is similar to steam that comes out from the volcano. While some vents are large, others are small, so one needs to be careful where one walks, as they are concealed under the grass all around the park.

It was in the advent of taking some images of these beauties that Peter heard Henry calling out for help repeatedly. Henry told Peter he wasn't too careful with his steps and tripped over some weeds. He found himself trapped in that steam vent, large enough to fit himself comfortably in.

Henry's hands were filled with slippery brown sulfur from the volcano that burned his hands. That's why it was hard for him to connect with his friend Peter. Henry was in panic mode, he was restless, and pushed the sides of the steam vent with his hands and the sulfur burnt him some more. He felt if he went lower into the vent, he'd surely vaporize from the lethal heat from the steam, or die by falling through the black hole leading to the volcano's boiling lava center.

And just when Henry thought he couldn't have it worse, his shoes slid off his feet into the heat beneath him. For a moment he was glad that happened, at least to save his feet from being cooked by melted rubber. But losing his shoes made the hot sulfur burn his soles through his socks. This mixture smelled worse than rotten eggs.

Soon came a man saying that help was coming for Henry, who was getting tired now after holding on and balancing for too long. Peter assured his friend Henry again, saying, "Hang in there pal, help is coming." Soon the team of chaperones arrived and formed a human chain, as that would prevent anyone from falling into the vent with Henry. That was how Henry was saved.

When Henry was pulled out and landed on the ground, he was stripped of his burning clothes so that the burns wouldn't get worse. Henry was naked in the presence of everyone and didn't care an inch. He was shaking and shivering from severe pain like he had never experienced all his life. Bottom line, he was grateful to be alive.

The stranger who helped earlier took Henry to paramedics. They first placed him in a sink of cold water so that his burns would not get worse. His temperature and blood pressure were taken and then he was transferred in an ambulance to a hospital. Henry kept telling the ambulance driver, "Please don't stop driving, just go." The pain was severe.

Henry's shock reduced after his first burn treatment, then he started to calm down for real. Henry confessed that if he had been alone when he fell into the steam vent, he would have died long ago. Friends are important to us in life. That statement couldn't be truer for Henry and many more of us who know the worth of human connection.

When Mark Lost Faith In His Gift

Be better at your craft

One day, the jolly fellow Mark Twain met a promising author named Frank on his return after a long walk with his German shepherd dog, and they both became friends. On one fateful day, Frank told Mark that he was losing his faith in his writing gift and inquired if Mark had ever gotten such a feeling before. To his amazement, Mark affirmed that the same feeling enveloped him fifteen years after he had been writing, and he felt he didn't have enough passion or talent for writing.

Mark Twain told Frank that he didn't give up writing, instead he got better at it. Mark expressly told Frank that life can make you feel that you are not enough by the struggles you are faced with or even make you feel you have chosen the wrong path, but keep your eyes on the ball and don't waver. Keep up with the efforts you are making towards your dream, because constant practice of your craft will make a master of you.

The Urgent Village Meeting And The Monk

Let every moment of your life count for something

One sunny day in a faraway village, members of the villa gathered to hold a public meeting. The main question in that meeting was if there was life after death. A monk at one side of the room laughed, but didn't contribute. When asked why he evaded the question he said, "Only those who have nothing tangible to do with their lives want another life that will last forever."

His disciples still questioned him, asking, "Is there life after death?" He answered, saying, "Is there life before death?" The monk's reply made them realize that they haven't been making the most of their lives, instead they have been worried about the "afterlife."

The burden of wondering if there is an afterlife is cumbersome. Live creatively and productively. Live life to serve others around you. We have to make the most of our lives while still on earth and stop bothering about another life thereafter.

The Eaglet-Chick Bird

Greatness resides within you

Once upon a time, Mr. Wisdom saw an abandoned eagle's egg by the wayside. He picked up the egg so it wouldn't get broken and placed it beneath a hen that was brooding her own eggs. After some time, the eaglet hatched and the chicken too. They all lived together, scampered for worms in the dirt together, and the eaglet acted like a chicken as it flew very little feet. Years later, the eaglet had grown into an eagle but still acted as a chicken. The eagle saw a magnificent bird gracefully flying in the sky and told the mother hen he wished he was able to glide with poise like that in the sky. The hen told him that they all belong to the ground while the gracious bird above, which is an eagle, belongs to the sky.

Moving with the wrong company is detrimental to growth. Taking advice from visionless people is limiting. It is best not to allow your past to predict your outcome and keep surrounding yourself with positive minded individuals.

Stop acting like a chicken. You are an eagle. Be mindful of your association. To a large extent, they can determine your outcome. As humans, we can only go as far as we believe we can.

Thomas Alva Edison And His Mean Teacher

You are not stupid, don't be silenced

Thomas Alva Edison was sent back home from school after his teacher told him he was too foolish to comprehend anything. He returned home downcast and told his mother all that transpired in school. She was heartbroken by this but she encouraged her son and decided to teach him going forward. Edison was self-taught and didn't attend any school or university. Many years later, he made history scientifically, with inventions such as the light bulb, electrographic vote-recorder, pneumatic stencil pen, magnetic ore-separator, the electric power meter, methods of preserving fruit, alkaline batteries for electric cars, concrete houses, concrete furniture, the phonograph for dolls and other toys, the spirit phone, etc.

Edison's teacher painted a false image of him. It was left for him to believe it or not. Edison's mum played a vital role in his life that erased the mindset his teacher attempted to build of him.

Guardians, parents, and elders have to be careful with how they respond to young people, as what they say can make or mar them. Every child is unique. Being self-taught isn't a taboo, and it has worked for many great minds today.

The Wise Boy From The Grocery Shop

Appraise your performance periodically

A long time ago, a young boy named Lawrence got into a grocery shop and rang a company number to inquire for the vacancy of an office boy. The receiver told Lawrence that a boy had assumed the position already recently and apologized to the young lad for better luck next time. Before Lawrence went off the phone, he asked the receiver if they were satisfied with the boy's services and she said yes. He smiled and went off the phone.

The owner of the grocery shop reached out to Lawrence and wondered why he was joyful that the position was taken. Lawrence replied that he was the boy who was employed a week ago and all he was doing was checking up.

It is good to treat another's business with a sense of ownership. Take ownership of the job handed to you, no matter how small it is.

Moses Scored An Own Goal!

We all make mistakes, learn from them

Moses ran as fast as his legs could carry him as he concentrated on the black and white object rotating ahead of him and knew that was his window to score a goal. This would be a dream come true for Moses. He looked behind and saw the yellow jerseys and green shorts of his teammates, the National Auto Glass Dinosaurs. Moses thought to himself as he smiled, They looked like a swarm of bees, all headed toward the soccer ball. Moses observed the faces of his opponents and it was easy to note that they were running very hard. But Moses said, "The ball is all mine!"

Moses kept chasing the ball and kicked it hard (as hard as a four-year-old can kick). It dashed far down the field, and he chased after the ball still. As the players got close to Moses, he was already very close to the goal post. Moses recognized that the goal keeper had a confused look as though he wasn't ready to save the ball. The rooting segment chanted, "Kick it! Kick the ball!"

Moses nervously kicked the ball hard and it bounced into the net. To his amazement, he had scored a goal – his first real goal! Moses ran back to his teammates, some cheered and many others crossed their hands in anger and with a heavy frown on their faces. Moses was sure that his other teammates were upset because they didn't have the opportunity he had to score the goal, but he did. Moses looked over at the sideline for his parents, who were laughing very hard with another parent. Moses felt cool about himself... he just scored his first goal, but for the other team!

We need to learn to celebrate our wins and failures, it teaches us how to do it better next time.

The Water Of Life And The Scorning Stones

Be diligent in the work committed into your hands

One day, a Spanish farmer felt very sick and was close to dying. A traveler told his entire family that he can be saved by the 'water of life' found on a mountaintop which is a three day journey. The stranger warned that as they climb the mountain, its stones will mock, shout, and jeer at them, but they are not to look at the stones or touch them. The family thanked the stranger and decided to embark on the journey.

The ill Spanish man had three sons and a daughter at the time, so his first son named Alonzo journeyed to the mountain and climbed. He heard the stones jeering and mocking him, but paid no attention to them. Almost getting to the top, one of the stones called Alonzo a bragger and a boastful person. He got upset and looked towards the stone and turned into a stone.

Weeks later, Carlo, the second son, embarked on the same quest to fetch the water of life to save their father's life and find his brother, but met the old man who advised them about the stones on the way up the mountain. Carlo climbed the mountaintop as the stones cried out, but he ignored them all.

Then, he heard his brother's voice and looked in that direction and turned into a stone.

One week after, Alfredo, the third son, went up the mountain, heard the stones crying out, and kept going up, singing and whistling along until he heard the melodious voice of a lady that attracted his attention. When he looked in that direction, he turned into stone.

His daughter, Evelyn, had no option than to summon courage and journey to the mountain for the water of life. Climbing up the mountain, Evelyn shut her ears to the noise the stones made and her eyes transfixed up the mountain and fetched the water of life into her goatskin until it was full. A few drops of the healing water touched a stone which turned into a man, so Evelyn sprinkled more all over the mountain and saved all those that have been trapped on the mountain for long, including her brothers.

On reaching the bottom of the mountain, Evelyn still had a lot more water of life for her father. The entire crowd celebrated her. When Maria got home, she gave her father the water of life which saved him.

Distractions will come to take your gaze off the prize. Make sure to keep your eyes fixed on your goal so that you can drown the noise around you.

Complete devotion and concentration are the solution. Don't respond to every insult or demeaning thing said to you, learn to look past it and focus on your goal. In a bid to do a good deed or carry out your God-given mandate, you will equally affect the lives of other people around you.

Life's Formula For Problems

Examine your life and fix yourself

One day, a priest was giving a sermon. He was popular for his sermons, as they were life changing. In his sermon, he asked what people would do if their vehicle broke down. The congregation answered and said that they would examine it and have it fixed. The priest asked again what they would do if their television set got spoiled, and they responded with the same response they gave earlier. So he later asked what they would do when their lives get faulty and need fixing. The congregation was startled and couldn't give him an answer.

When life gets faulty, we fail to examine and correct what needs to be addressed, so improvement keeps dragging on. Everything will not always go as planned in life. It is only normal.

Get more functional and intentional with your life. Take good care of yourself and stop looking for strange formulas to solve all your problems. Begin to examine your life choices.

An Almost Obese Coach

Be willing to change, don't be rigid

Anthony Robbins was born by a loose mum that had many partners, which exposed him to different father figures that were all infidels and poverty-stricken men. Today, Anthony Robbins is a life coach, but his earlier life was difficult.

As a teenager, Anthony worked with John Grinder and helped him to promote his content on Neuro Linguistic Programming. While working to cajole people to attend John's seminars and read his outputs, he persuaded John to train him on the nitty-gritties of his field. John obliged. This made Anthony a millionaire at a young age.

In his early 20's, his physical activity was nothing to write home about, and that made him gain so much weight. This affected his career, but with the help of his friend who pushed him, his life turned around for good. Anthony got back on his feet. With the past behind him, he worked on himself and is now a renowned life coach with helpful books to his name like Giant Steps, the Unlimited Power, Notes from a Friend, and Awaking the Giant Within.

Anthony has a Mastery University for self-help and has accepted many participants in his educational facility. He holds self-improvement meetings on acquiring and managing wealth and achieving a healthy lifestyle. His experience has brought him before the House of Commons and House of the Lords. Not only that, he has also worked hand in hand with many notable people like Andre Agassi, Mother Teresa, Michael Douglas, and Princess Diana, just to mention a few.

Your past doesn't equal your future. Always surround yourself with real friends who will tell you the truth no matter what. This is what helped Anthony today, as his friend helped him back into his graceful reality. Now, he is a household name.

World's Greatest Basketballer

Leave an indelible mark in your generation

Who is the world's greatest basketballer? Did you say Michael Jordan? If yes, then you guessed right...

Michael Jordan was born in 1963 in Brooklyn, New York. He is a living basketball icon. He is known globally as the world's greatest basketball player. His nicknames are "Air Jordan" and "His Airness." MJ had great precision as he played and he is 6'6" in stature with outstanding scoring abilities. During the regular season, he scored thirty three points on average and during the playoffs, he scored thirty points on average.

In 1984, during the National Basketball Association's season, he was picked as number 3 and began making headlines. He won Rookie of the Year and made moves for the Chicago Bulls. He played professionally for five seasons in 1990 and was responsible for the three straight wins of the Chicago Bulls. Later, the team bagged three more championship trophies, all thanks to MJ.

In 1988, this highly sought after basketballer was crowned the best defensive player and awarded as the "Most Valuable

Player," which was crested into the Basketball Hall of Fame. MJ was the pride of the NBA All-Star Games and the American Olympics.

MJ was rejected into Emsley A. Laney High School's basketball varsity team during his sophomore year because he wasn't of the required height nor skill yet. That singular act jolted him and he kept practicing to be better. His zeal for basketball was evident for all to see. He trained hard and was accepted into the varsity team, but just as a team member. He got discouraged and felt underutilized, but his faith never wavered for once.

With every rejection MJ got, he practiced even harder. He got a position in the junior basketball team in school and qualified for a college basketball scholarship. MJ got basketball scholarship grants from the University of North Carolina and others, which he accepted as a skilled basketballer as he studied cultural geography in school.

MJ later left college to join the NBA during his junior year and came back to finish his studies. MJ was tenacious. He didn't take no for an answer. For every young person with a dream, keep practicing and honing your skill diligently and the sky will just be your starting point.

The Playground That Changed The Narrative

Turn your disaster into opportunities

Dave Richmond called out to Charles. "Charles, we're going to the store to get biscuits. Do you want to come along?" It was a Sunday afternoon in July. Charles accompanied his friends as they walked, chatting away carefree, along some blocks to the store. They crossed the railroad tracks, kicking empty cans, and slightly throwing rocks as they walked.

Charles was the sixth child of eight kids. He was eight years old, a second-grader living with his mother in the housing project, some blocks from the train tracks.

Charles was a country body who resided in the country for the most part of his life. Their small town of Millen appeared as a giant playground to him. Charles and his friends loved to stroll and tour. Cargo trains were a daily norm in their small town. The trains would offload and collect boxcars and tank cars at the loading yards, then head on to Savannah. It was established that the tracks were between Charles's home, the church, the store, and their neighborhood. Charles and his friends would often get a chance to jump over them.

Charles was an energetic child who loved sports. The other kids loved him because he was fun to be with. He always had a smile on his face. Charles feared nothing and was ready to face any situation his friends brought along.

On this cold day, Charles despised wearing his jacket, so he went out that chilly day without it. All he wore was a short-sleeved shirt with his jeans and tennis shoes. On the way home from the store, Charles and his friends started playing on a cargo train that stopped to drop off and pick up items. Close to the middle of the cargo train, these boys were having so much fun as they ran on and off the ladder train. It was exhilarating and a wonder to be on a moving train, to hear the screeching of the wheels as it came to a stop with its loud whistle blowing, and then the euphoria to experience the sounds and tangs of the engine as the train moved to and fro.

The train started moving forward on the tracks, and all the boys alighted the train, except Charles. Charles yelled out to his friends, telling them, "I'll get down at the next stop. You all meet me there." Charles' intention was to drop off at the dirt railroad just outside of town, which wasn't far off. This was a feat they have all been looking forward to and would have a great laugh about.

At that time, the wind started getting cold, but Charles held tightly to the ladder behind the cargo train. Just ahead, was the dirt railroad he was to drop off at, but at this point the cargo train began to pick up speed. The cargo train passed the dirt stop he should have dropped off from and he knew it was a bad idea to jump off now because the train was moving too fast.

All of a sudden, Charles became very cold from the wind and fright. The adventure he craved was no longer fun, but he held on tightly. He prayed and waited for the lights to the next town so that he would get off and ask for help to get back home. It was very cold and Charles said to himself, "If my jacket was here, I would definitely wear it now. I am so cold."

Charles' hands started freezing. The area the train traveled had many bushes, and his hope came alive on seeing houses and some lights ahead. But unfortunately, the cargo train kept on moving! Now Charles began to fear for real. He thought to himself, "Should I just jump. How long do I have to wait till the train reaches its destination?" But it was very dangerous to jump, so he decided to just hold on until the train stopped.

For each village they passed, Charles got more scared, and his faith dwindled the more. He tried to encourage himself as tears of agony flowed down his cold cheeks, saying, "Hold on tight buddy, you can do this. Soon you'll be home and you will wear your jacket and everything will be warm and cozy."

Now Charles was exhausted. It was getting dark, as the sun had set. Maybe he should just jump and bear whatever consequences came with it. Back at home, Charles' friends didn't want to get into trouble, so they kept that event a secret until Charles was discovered missing. Then they spilled. The police began to look for Charles, while family, friends, and strangers searched by air, rail, and on foot. Five days after Charles' adventure on the train, he was found dead along a deserted stretched rail many miles down the rail track.

Charles died from a broken neck; the community was aggrieved at his death. The news covered this incident and recounted that there was no playground for children in Millen. On hearing this, a lady in Savannah (a past girl Scout troop leader) was extremely sad and thought to herself, If there had been a playground in Millen, then children would not have to play on the train track and such a tragic event like this could have been avoided. This lady from Savannah vowed to build a playground for kids in Millen. The people of Millen came together and erected a new playground in Millen for kids. This process of building the playground ignited a bond amongst strangers who later became friends. Healing occurred in the community that reduced their sorrow.

Soichiro The Patient Chap

Hard work rewards in countless folds

Once upon a time, a child was born to a blacksmith who owned a bicycle repair shop. The child was named Soichiro Honda, and he loved to be in his father's blacksmith shop because he was born to love tinkering. So, he visited his father's shop, mostly to enhance his tinkering passion. As the world evolved, Soichiro got more enticed by technology, especially during the emergence of manufacturing at the time that moved the gaze of the world from agriculture.

When Soichiro was sixteen years old, formal education wasn't pleasurable to him, so he stopped schooling and applied to Tokyo's automobile servicing companies. Soichiro worked for free at the Art Shokai in Tokyo as a mechanic intern, which is a company that services cars that need maintenance and repairs.

Soichiro Honda is the brain behind Honda Motors Company. He wasn't born into wealth, his parents were a blacksmith and a weaver, but he had an inborn desire for machinery. Once, he pursued a car down the street just because of the engine oil emitting from it. It thrilled him to his very core.

All Soichiro was given at his place of apprenticeship was a bed to sleep on and food. He continued to improve on his craft and took special attention to the cars given to him to fix. In the shortest time, he had become more competent in maintaining and repairing cars.

Soichiro grew more creative by the day. He simplified difficult repair methods to make the job easier. His passion for invention grew as well. He handled automotive tools in the most supernatural of ways that many couldn't comprehend.

In his spare time, he was busy reading motorcycling publications and memorizing every detail of it. Soon he became educated in machinery. The managers of Art Shokai saw Soichiro's dedication and commitment and rewarded him by teaching him everything he knows about the business and machinery.

His abilities were employed during times of manufacturing vehicles. At the age of twenty two, he had started making high-end spare parts using eccentric means. Soichiro took to the race tracks as an associate engineer. He later had full autonomy to oversee Art Shokai's subsidiary close to his home. At this time, he was the most sought after mechanic in the land and was very successful.

He had to leave Art Shokia when his idea to begin the manufacturing of piston rings was rejected. Then he began his own business of making piston rings. He went back to school to get a better understanding of metals before venturing into the manufacturing of piston rings. He supplied Toyota and Japan's automotive giants. The war broke out and he was no longer the president of his company, but just an operations manager. Most of the men were recruited into the army, leaving mostly women in the helm of affairs in his company. He altered the manufacturing procedure to make it easier for the women to adopt, and things moved on smoothly until there was a bombing by the American warplanes that took down the building holding his piston rings and other machineries.

The war affected his business greatly, as he had to sell off what he could salvage from the war to Japan's big companies so he could survive. Then the demand for motor vehicles brought about the Honda Motor Company. He first made the Honda motorcycle in 1948, which won several global motorcycle races.

He was discouraged from car manufacturing by the Department of Trade then, because they feared another automotive company would crowd the market, but Soichiro continued working on his model and built a more compact but efficient model that was a perfect fit for the season.

Failure didn't stop Soichiro from living his dream, that's why we have the Honda motorcycles, cars, marine, and aerospace parts and equipment. Honda is still one of the leading automotive manufacturers whose products are still winning races globally.

Patience is a rare virtue present in every great mind and this virtue helped Soichiro a great deal. Soichiro was a detailed and analytical thinker. He didn't take chances with his creations. He always studied and made sure he got it right at all times.

Soichiro kept evolving with the times and seasons. He was abreast of every new invention and learnt them all.

Unfortunately, the war broke out, but it birthed the Honda Motor Company today.

The Only Self-Taught President

Don't let your circumstance define you

Abraham Lincoln was born in 1809 to his parents Thomas and Nancy Lincoln, in a small log cabin in Kentucky. He had a terrible childhood and didn't have an ideal education befitting a President. Abraham's childhood didn't deter him from becoming a great President as history will have it.

Abraham Lincoln was the 16th President of the U.S, but he faced several stumbling blocks en route to his dream to becoming president. Misfortune struck when his family moved to Indiana. They faced the milk sickness that killed his mother and many other of his family members.

At a young age, Abraham had to be responsible for himself and his sister. He had to leave school to help at home. He started training himself at home, and this was the same way he got his law degree.

When Abraham was old enough, he moved out of his family home to begin his own life in New Salem, Illinois, where he worked at a store. Moving to New Salem contributed hugely to his personal development in the area of speaking and persuasion. Abraham kept developing himself, read widely, met different individuals daily, and kept borrowing books to learn about the law practice, as he couldn't afford one.

He used the knowledge he gathered for public office. His walk into presidency wasn't a walk in the park, he served in the Illinois Militia as a captain of the troop during the Black Hawk War. His first attempt as a candidate of the Illinois Legislature was unsuccessful but was later re-elected and won. He served for four terms in office and used this opportunity to perfect his law studies.

Another political attempt at furthering his position in the Congress flopped, so he focused on law by representing people who needed help with monetary disputes, transportation issues, and even murder charges, which he did for about fifteen years.

The love of Abraham's life, Ann Rutledge, died of Typhoid fever in 1835, when he engaged her to be married to him. He later married Mary Todd after they had earlier broken their scheduled wedding date two years before. Abraham had four sons and lost three of them. The first son, Edward, died of tuberculosis at three, the second son William died at eleven, and the fourth son, Thomas, died of heart failure at eighteen. Only Robert Todd lived healthy until he passed at the age of eighty two.

His wife, Mary, was psychologically and emotionally unstable. She had to be taken to a mental health facility for the later part of her life. Abraham, on the other hand, struggled from severe depression and for six months he had to be watched closely at home.

The reemerging cases of slavery in the U.S made Abraham run for public office again. He became famous with his response about disagreeing with the proposition to trade slaves in the U.S. and then the entrance of the Republican Party also empowered his chances to being in the Senate.

He later became the 16th President of the U.S., but his vision to abolish slavery was unpopular. His rule and his actions irked the system. There was a Civil War as a result. This broke the nation and seven states came together to make their own country uniting against Abraham's leadership – the Confederate States of America. Slaves were later freed during his rule by his decree. His military skill and vast political knowledge won the Confederate States over to the United States.

During his reign as president, the Civil War came to an end and he ruled a second term, but his life was cut short at the end of the Civil War. Abraham's legacy lives on, and America is a free nation where race and gender is not a predetermining factor whether a person is worthy to live or a gauge of social status.

The African Slave Prince

You have what it takes to lead

There was an African prince named Toussaint L'Ouverture who was captured by the French and taken to Haiti from Africa in the late 1600s, amongst other black people. They were forcefully captured at the time.

Toussaint was liked and trusted by his master and was granted his freedom when he got to thirty three years old. He used his liberty to fight the evil called slavery and began an army of like minds to free slaves from captivity. They achieved the "Haitian Revolution" as the army freed many slaves few years later. His dedication to the cause helped him free the slaves quicker than expected, as they have been enslaved for hundreds of years.

Dedication is required in any course you find yourself doing. Toussaint was a compassionate leader whose love for humanity transcended the norm. Being a leader means sacrificing for them and doing so in love.

Malcolm X Turns A New Leaf

Learn from your mistakes

Since Malcolm X was born, his family was threatened and harassed constantly by racists, and they had to keep moving from one place to the other to evade the violence. It was during this time that Earl (Malcom's father) was murdered in cold blood as a racist move, though the police were adamant at accepting this reality.

Malcolm's mum broke down due to this loss and this made her unable to take proper care of Malcolm and his other siblings. Thus, they had to move into foster homes. Later, Malcolm had to reside in a juvenile detention center, but he still did well in his studies in school.

Malcolm got weary at a point due to many challenges faced. He got worse when a teacher told him he would never make it to college, and this led him to drop out of school. Coming out of school opened him up to unlawful dealings that made him end up in prison. In prison, he started studying again and swore to change his life.

Out of prison, Malcolm X turned into a captivating speaker whose speeches are still cited to date. He also became one of the greatest civil rights leaders history has ever had.

Albert The Selfless Traditional Chief

You matter

Once upon a time, there was a selfless man named Albert John Luthuli. He lived in South Africa during the times when SA was a hard place to live, as Black people were treated unjustly and were refused equal living. Albert, being a courageous man, played a crucial role in the history of South Africa.

Albert spearheaded a human right fight with other black people. He became the first African to win a Nobel Peace Prize because he devoted his life to helping humanity. This political leader was an extraordinary model to many young people, but he had a rough childhood.

Losing his father at a tender age worsened his chances for a better life. His mum had to toil as a washerwoman to feed Albert and herself. Albert's family were traditional people to the core and he was trained in school by the family chiefs. He turned out to be a teacher and embarked on some missionary work. He chose to become a chief himself as that was an avenue to positively affect his people further.

Albert fought to make South Africa a saner and equal place to live in for all. He abandoned his passion for teaching to serve his community. You are special and you have a divine purpose to accomplish on earth.

The Learned Slave Boy

Don't be afraid to face your fears

A long time ago, there lived a boy named Frederick Douglass who began to learn how to read at twelve years old as a slave. He summoned courage and taught other slaves, but that process was truncated by the slave masters who were threatened by the intelligence and quick eloquence of the slaves.

Frederick Douglass was an abolitionist who fought hard to put an end to slavery. Abolitionists were the heroes that fought to end slavery. Frederick advocated for the equal rights of black men and women and to end slavery in America.

Frederick Douglas spent most of his life championing the rights of black people and women. He fought hard to abolish slavery in America and to end the unequal treatment of women.

Later, Frederick escaped from slavery with the help of a free-born black woman he loved from Baltimore, and they got married afterwards.

Frederick spoke up on the eradication of slavery in spite of the strife the subject matter was bringing amongst people of different races. He further established some newspapers to help spread his message on ending slavery and proper education backing his claim.

Only a selfless person could have achieved all that Frederick did, so he had to become altruistic for the gain of the people. He applied patience in all he did and achieved.

Frederick spoke up courageously on the abolition of the menace called slavery. He was keen on passing his knowledge to his people. This is an attribute we all should emulate. Let's not be comfortable being the only smart or enlightened ones amongst a group.

The Champion With A Speech Defect

Dream big and keep working at it until you succeed

A long time ago, a son was born to a former dancer and hairdresser. He was named Michael Sylvester Gardenzio Stallone on July 6, 1946. He had nerve damage that resulted during the time of his birth due to the difficulty his mother (Jackie) experienced while birthing him, and tongs were used to bring him to the world. This struggle affected Sylvester Stallone. That's why he has an incoherent speech and a funny accent.

Sylvester Stallone was brought up in a hostile setting where his parents fought so much and later divorced. He wasn't shown love by his parents, was body shamed by his mother, and called a brainless child by his father. He struggled in his studies and was emotionally starved of his folks.

His school expelled him thrice and he was later put in foster home after his parent's divorce. Much later, he had to be taken to a special school for troubled kids. He became better and decided to help other children passing through similar pain as he once did.

He decided to become an actor and studied drama at the Miami State University and moved to New York shortly after due to his overwhelming desire for the craft. Agents denied him roles in acting as he was said not to be acting material. His wife also cajoled him to get a real job, but he was still focused on his dream. He took any little acting role just to make ends meet, even a pornographic role. His wife kept fighting him as she was tired of their poor situation and wanted a break so badly.

Stallone developed a love for writing, storytelling, and fed it by visiting the city library, often to write stories and scripts of ill situations turning out great just as his own is. At his lowest point, he had to sell his dog. Inspired by the great Muhammad Ali and the story of Rocky Balboa, Stallone wrote a manuscript and offered it to Robert Chartoff and Irwin Winkler, who were casting for a production. They were impressed with the script and bought the manuscript off him and allowed him to play the role of Rocky, even though they objected at first.

In 1976, Rocky was published and the public received the movie well. He made a lot of money even though he was still nursing his wounds at the time of release. This opened him up to his career in writing, acting, and directing. The rest is history!

The Rare Rock Club

Change the world if you don't like the way it is

Many years ago, when Marian Wright Edelman was in second grade, she was watching the news with her family one night and remembered seeing a group of homeless people sleeping outside in the cold. This image haunted her for long, she felt so sorry for them, and desired to help them. She expressed her desire to her folks and her father responded, "You are very little, what can you do?"

When Marian got back to school, she opened a club to help raise funds for the homeless, which she called the Rock Club. When she started initially, they had only five members, but soon there were twenty. People joined easily and the club grew.

During their free time at recess, they painted rocks, animals, flowers, shapes, and sports teams. Marian and her team went round searching for teachers and adults who would buy their rocks to use as paperweights.

These rocks were sold for five cents, ten cents, and even up to five dollars. By Christmas, they were able to raise thirty-three dollars and they gave it to a local homeless shelter.

Marian's mom took her and her friend to the homeless shelter to give the money. When they arrived, several complete families laid on the snowy sidewalk, looking sad and hungry. Entering the building and walking up to the receptionist, Marian delivered the money to her and she expressed her sincere gratitude for their donation. The receptionist offered to tour the building, which they agreed to do. There were many rows of over one hundred tables arranged for feeding. In the kitchen, the helpers seemed to be baking endless rows of gingerbread men so that it was enough to feed the present and intended homeless people that would walk into the premises.

After touring the building, Marian saw a homeless man by the snow-filled pavement. He wore a very dirty green coat and black pants that were covered in mud. He held tightly to a Christmas tree, ornamented with red accessories. Marian felt very sorry for the homeless man, because even in his state, he recognized the season and still celebrated it in his own way.

The following day, an image of this homeless man was in the newspapers. This image resonated with many people and made them realize that homeless people need to be cared for in and out of season. After a few days, some reporters invaded Marian's school for an image of their Rock Club members. The next day, an article with an image to go with was in the newspapers. Marian and her team were very pleased by their act.

Marian's school took initiative to begin a program for children. Now the kids at the school help homeless people and contribute their quota to the needy. It's funny how just painting a few rocks and some caring children made a huge difference in our world.

Arnold Schwarzenegger, My True Hero

Go the extra mile

Arnold Alois Schwarzenegger began his career as a bodybuilder. He started lifting weights at fifteen-years-old. He competed for Mr. Universe at twenty years old and Mr. Olympia, and won those titles five times and seven times respectively. Although the path to this success wasn't an easy one, he is now a movie star and politician.

Arnold suffered from unequal treatment from his father, Gustav Schwarzenegger, who believed that Arnold wasn't his biological child, and doted on his older brother instead. He was from a traditional Austrian family that struggled to make ends meet. In fact, getting a refrigerator was the highest achievement of their family.

Arnold's father was a policeman who gave him a tough childhood. He was forced to excel at sports, especially soccer. Arnold was physically abused by his dad, which was accepted as a custom in Austria then. It became harder for him when his mother passed. Now there would be no one to comfort him and assure him that everything would be just fine.

To leave that abusive life behind, move to America, and live the wealthy life he had always dreamed of, he knew he had to do well at soccer and leave his family home. So he took his workouts very seriously in spite of the heart condition he was born with. Arnold suffered from a condition called bicuspid aortic valve, meaning he was born with two valves instead of three. This causes poor oxygen circulation and heightened stress on the heart. But Arnold kept working out until he won Mr. Junior Europe, which opened up his other winnings thereafter, because he focused on his bodybuilding career.

As Arnold became more popular, he moved to London to pursue his bodybuilding career and lived with his personal trainer's family and learnt to speak English. This helped his dream of becoming an actor. He made money from several competitions and moved to America in 1968 to achieve his dreams, but he had to keep working at it and trained harder. He acted in some low budget movies until his break in his bodybuilding career that brought him world record winnings that ushered him to be on bodybuilding platforms to give commentaries on the same subject matter to the younger generation. He also wrote a book and had his articles in many magazines on sport.

It wasn't until Arnold retired that his big break came in the 1980s with the movie Conan the Barbarian, which showed off his acting prowess to its full. Afterwards, he was featured in more movies like the Terminator, Predator, the Expendables (part 1 & 2), and True Lies, just to mention a few.

Under the Republican Party, Arnold later became the Governor of California for two terms and was rumored to want to run for presidency at the time. This story teaches us to be steadfast on what we believe in, because the realization of your dream will surely see the light of day, no matter how long it takes. So, it's best to set realistic goals. Arnold is proof that one can be self-taught and emerge great.

The Self-Made Man

Self-control

George Washington is popularly known as the "Self-made man and the Father of America." This able commander-in-chief commanded the well-trained General of the American advance forces nicknamed "boiling water" – Charles Lee to go strike down Sir Henry Clinton's bigger British force which was on their way from Philadelphia to New York.

Lee, being a stubborn man, almost rejected the command to intercept the British in New Jersey, but later agreed. Lee approached the battle with the utmost inhumane display for human life and disorder. When the commander-in-chief reached the battle front to check on how well his troops were doing, what Washington saw shook him to his core and churned out a Washington attribute which was rumored home and abroad but rarely encountered: his enormous rage.

Lee's incompetence vexed Washington, who lost his self-control over how the Americans were about to be defeated at the hands of the British because of Charles Lee's lack of precision. George Washington took over the order of the battle for the Americans and ordered Lee out of the battle front. He encouraged his fellow soldiers to stand firm, not retreat, but approach their enemy, the British.

Washington's magnificent courage rubbed off the American troops, who took over the battle of Monmouth Courthouse, all thanks to Washington's strong will that was formed in fervent disposition that he tamed by a high degree of self-control. His rare display of discipline and composure has been spoken of till date, as how he salvaged America from its enemies into a safe and sane era worthy of accolades.

Washington, at the age of twenty two, offered to serve as a soldier in an upcoming conflict with the French, which invaded and claimed lands in places far from the Appalachians, which the British crown claimed for theirs and called Ohio. With no military experience, Washington was honored with the rank of lieutenant colonel and marched at the head of two companies of Virginia militia into Pennsylvania. This means he'd join Britain's Indian allies and face the French at Ft. Duquesne, which is situated at the site of the future city of Pittsburgh.

Washington exuded more discipline during the battle in the Pennsylvanian wilderness. Soon, he was promoted to the position of a colonel in the army. He ordered the first shots fired in the French and Indian War, the first theater of the first truly world war – the Seven Years' War, which proved that this young Virginian would churn out a man of great importance. He fortified his army and prepared them to face Ft. Duquesne's French army. But they faced a humbling defeat at their hands, because their enemies had an advantage of the terrain of the chosen battle field.

Another scenario where Washington showcased his courage and astute connectedness was when he was ill with dysentery and General Braddock (he made Washington his aide) was ambushed by nine hundred French and Indian soldiers along the Monongahela River. Still, Washington got up from his sick bed into the battlefield. The battle wasn't won, but he helped to bring orders to the battle, and with his help, the entire army of Virginia was extinguished.

In 1759, Washington resigned, continuing as colonel to be a brigadier general, assumed a position at the Virginia legislature and the House of Burgesses, and also married a rich widow named Martha Dandridge Curtis.

Washington's mastery of self-control formed his character and he grew more mature. This affected his sense of judgment and leadership, which benefited the country a great deal.

Washington learnt to govern himself before he presided over his great nation that he was also a subject to. He was undaunted and faced his fears courageously. His humbling defeat didn't tarnish his progressing reputation among Virginians. His reputation was more important to him than accomplishments.

The Worries Of A Loving Father

Hopeful

A man named John Winthrop was a dedicated Puritan and a great father whose thought was always with his children due to the corrupting church and mundane temptations enveloping England at the time. He feared mostly for his second son, Henry, who exuded habits that were forbidden by the devout Puritans. Worse still, Henry got married to his cousin Bess, but was still irresponsible and immature.

At this time, the Puritans feared that their influence would never bring back righteousness to England, godliness to the Anglican Church, and inspire the community to live faithfully in covenant with God.

John Winthrop later abandoned the security his nation brought to live in an unknown land just to form the mannerism of a new civilization somewhere in America. Winthrop moved out of England due to the disregard of Puritans, the Anglican Church, and the ungodly and unchaste behavior of the then King Charles.

Some investors came together to form the Massachusetts Bay Company in 1629 to show support to an English settlement in America for the provision of tobacco, furs, and many other communities for trading. Winthrop noticed that such company's charter are always authorized by the king, but in the Massachusetts Bay Company charter, it didn't make provisions for their operations to be overseen by a board of directors in England. This oversight wasn't noticed by the king or his ministers, but Winthrop noticed that loophole. The charter needed to be adjusted so that the company wouldn't have sole autonomy to do as they please when they came to America.

Winthrop used this fine medium to establish a colony that governs its own financial and political affairs and could also enforce the tenets of God and men's laws. New England would have faithful's who would build and keep a new covenant with God that was free from the wayward priests, heretics, and the king's influence. So Winthrop, in a collision with the Massachusetts Bay Company, hit the ground running as they sourced for funds and manpower to build a new society. Winthrop saw this as a divine intervention and prepared for it.

Settlers in New England were mostly Puritans and a handful of non-Puritans who emigrated for economic reasons and were skilled in building. Winthrop was appointed to govern the new enterprise. Four ships sailed on April 7, 1630, carrying four hundred settlers of the initial Massachusetts Bay Company for the New World. Later, six hundred more sailed after. Winthrop moved out of England with Henry, his second son, and they sailed with other Puritan emigrants on the Arabella. Winthrop left England with the sole aim of propagating the gospel in the New World and to live by the instructions in the Bible.

The journey was tedious. Many lost hope, some fell ill and died, while Winthrop's hope was still alive. On arrival, the settlers were weak, hungry, and sea sick. They built new huts and cultivated fields for food. They met the local Native Americans who taught them how to live in the wild.

Later, his family joined him in New England, a countless number of new settlers came and built the greatest civilization in history.

Learn to be wise, compassionate, and upright. To lead, you have to lead by example. You have to serve first before you become a leader.

The Wealthy Blind Writer

Steadfastness

Once there lived a prolific writer named Eric Hoffer. People believed that his every thought was penned down in his books and notes. Eric buttressed the purpose of liberty at every opportunity given. Born in 1902, Eric was born to German immigrant parents, with no formal education nor did he get married. This loner was a successful author who was financially buoyant due to his skillful writing.

His writing tone is often unsentimental, dark, regulated, and cool. He didn't acquire any property, even though he could afford it. Eric left us with the thoughts and the wisdom we need to comprehend the possibilities for good and evil in you and I, and also the communities we shape. Eric spent ample time enhancing and expressing various opinions on human nature. His humbling personality was enviable and rare in the midst of the plenty he had, and he loved to be addressed as an ordinary longshoreman.

He proudly called himself a misfit living in America built by fellow misfits. He turned blind at seven years old and had to bear his father's scorn after his mother died. His father called him an idiot child and hired a caregiver named Martha Bauer for blind Eric. Eric exuded joy in spite of his blindness, an unloving father, and the fact that most of them in the family don't seem to live past the age of forty. So, he was advised by his nanny countless times to make the most of his life while young.

At fifteen years old, Eric got his sight restored out of nowhere and he pounded into writing for fear of losing it mysteriously again. He was always in the library and finished reading the contents in most libraries. He lost his father after World War I and had to fend for himself.

He attempted suicide but failed to swallow the poison because it tasted awful, and moved to California to live a wandering life. Eric Hoffer continued reading regardless. One of the books he read that inspired him to do the same about his life was Essays of a sSixteenth-century French Philosopher Named Michel de Montaigne. The book represented the author's experiences, desires, travels, delights, disappointments, observations, opinion, and mannerism of others to get to some truth relating to mankind.

Eric began to write about his observations of mankind in his notebooks. He would dress in his working man clothes, reside by the road, read, think, and write all he observed about human behavior – this made him a philosopher. His study of human nature formed the theme of his popular book, the Impulses in People Which Attracts Them to Mass Movements. He discovered that it was the absence of self-esteem that caused individuals to give in to mass movements, just as Russians and Germans embraced the evil results of surrendering to Stalin and Hitler.

He found out that in America, it was the need for accomplishment, the spirit of leaders who made something worthy for themselves out of nothing, that gave people their sense of their own self-worth, desire to achieve more for themselves and their nation as a whole. He published his first book, the True Believer, in 1951. Eric Hoffer's book was a great success. It showed why humans are attracted to Nazism and communism movements, Islamic extremists, and other movements that disregard and disdain human life. So people join a mass movement to evade personal responsibility or be 'free from freedom' – like a Nazi puts it.

Eric was a fine mouthpiece for Americans, not educated but had read so much and written intelligently over the years about the outcasts who made it possible in America to give us freedom. His books went global and fetched him good money, even President Eisenhower cheered him as his favorite author. He had a column in a newspaper, held offices at the University of California at Berkeley and at Stanford University about the truths of human nature and societies.

Eric had always wanted to work at the dock as a longshoreman before he passed, but he was getting too old for that sort of physically demanding job. Nevertheless, he continued thinking and brainstorming. He gave up his column and decided to go low until he passed in 1983.

A life filled with crisis, disappointments, achievements, surprises, and different turns is a monumental life indeed.

Conclusion

As Boys we face so many huddles in life, but when we develop the spirit of not giving up, there is nothing we can't achieve in life. Nothing is impossible for a boy who have this Magic – not giving up. Take the first step, if its not working, try again, it always seems impossible until it's done.

Always have a winning mindset because winners never quit and quitters never win.

Made in the USA
Monee, IL
07 July 2026